HOLD HANDS

SARA VARON

First Second
New York

For Sheila, Nora, Miles & Eily

Very big thanks to Richard Simon and
Sheila O'Donnell For their writing help.

First Second

Copyright © 2019 by Sara Varon

Published by First Second
First Second is an imprint oF Roaring Brook Press, a division oF Holtzbrinck Publishing Holdings Limited Partnership
175 FiFth Avenue, New York, NY 10010

Don't miss your next Favorite book From First Second!
For the latest updates go to Firstsecondnewsletter.com and signup For our enewsletter.

Library oF Congress Control Number: 2018944891

ISBN: 978-1-59643-588-9

Our books may be purchased in bulk For promotional, educational, or business use. Please contact your local bookseller or the macmillan Corporate
and Premium Sales Department at (800) 221-7945 ext. 5442 or by e-mail at MacmillanSpecialMarkets@macmillan.com.

FIRST
EDITION

First edition, 2019
Book design by Andrew Arnold
Printed in China by Toppan LeeFung Printing Ltd., Dongguan City, Guangdong Province

1 3 5 7 9 10 8 6 4 2

Hold hands
when the day is new,

when you need a pal,

or when one needs you.

Hold hands
beFore pancakes

and during cheese.

Hold hands to steady your trembling knees.

Hold hands each time you cross the street.

Hold hands when you say goodbye,

and also when you're jumping high.

Hold hands with your buddy when you're on the go,

especially if your teacher tells you so.

Hold hands on a ledge, on a bridge, in a hedge.

You can even hold hands with a tree instead.

Hold hands **going out.**

Hold hands getting in.

Hold hands when you go to a friend's to play,

and when it's time to
be on your way.

Hold hands with your brother and your sister too.

Hold hands with your mother when she kisses you.